Not Again

Jack Gabolinscy
Brian Harrison

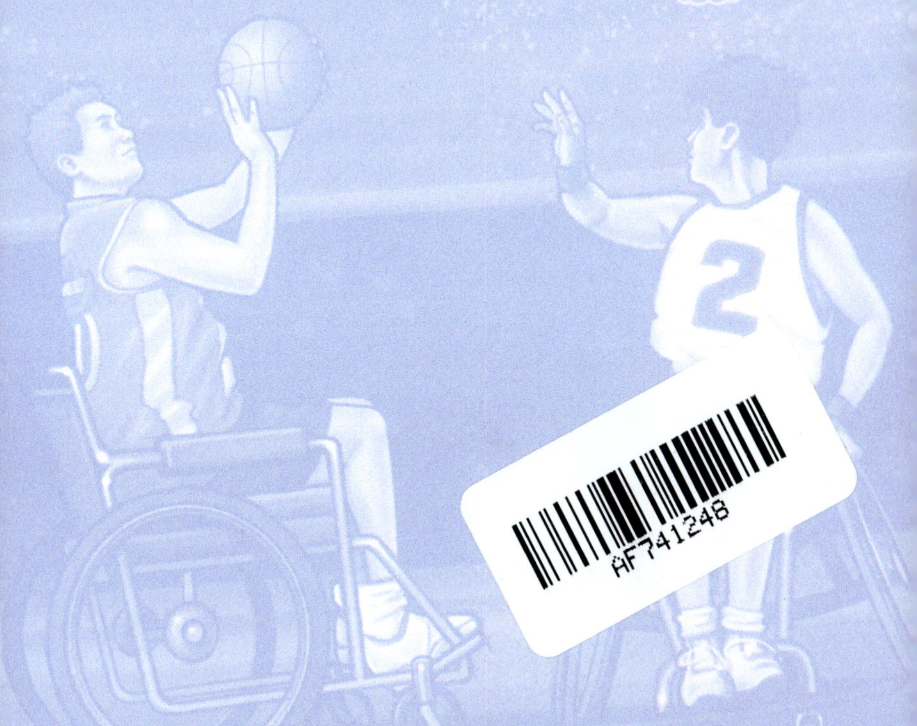

NELSON
CENGAGE Learning™

Australia • Brazil • Japan • Korea • Mexico • Singapore • Spain • United Kingdom • United States

NELSON
CENGAGE Learning

Not Again

Fast Forward
Emerald Level 25

Text: Jack Gabolinscy
Illustrations: Brian Harrison
Design: Ami Sharpe
Series design: James Lowe
Production controller: Seona Galbally
Audio recordings: Juliet Hill, Picture Start
Spoken by: Matthew King and Abbe Holmes

Text © 2008 Cengage Learning Australia Pty Limited
Illustrations © 2008 Cengage Learning Australia Pty Limited

Copyright Notice
This Work is copyright. No part of this Work may be reproduced, stored in a retrieval system, or transmitted in any form or by any means without prior written permission of the Publisher. Except as permitted under the Copyright Act 1968, for example any fair dealing for the purposes of private study, research, criticism or review, subject to certain limitations. These limitations include: Restricting the copying to a maximum of one chapter or 10% of this book, whichever is greater; Providing an appropriate notice and warning with the copies of the Work disseminated; Taking all reasonable steps to limit access to these copies to people authorised to receive these copies; Ensuring you hold the appropriate Licences issued by the Copyright Agency Limited ("CAL"), supply a remuneration notice to CAL and pay any required fees.

ISBN 978 0 17 012721 9
ISBN 978 0 17 012717 2 (set)

Cengage Learning Australia
Level 7, 80 Dorcas Street
South Melbourne, Victoria Australia 3205
Phone: 1300 790 853

Cengage Learning New Zealand
Unit 4B Rosedale Office Park
331 Rosedale Road, Albany, North Shore NZ 0632
Phone: 0508 635 766

For learning solutions, visit cengage.com.au

Printed in China by 1010 Printing International Ltd
3 4 5 6 7 8 12 11 10 09

POSTERA CRESCAM LAUDE
THE UNIVERSITY OF MELBOURNE

Evaluated in independent research by staff from the Department of Language, Literacy and Arts Education at the University of Melbourne.

Not Again

Jack Gabolinscy
Brian Harrison

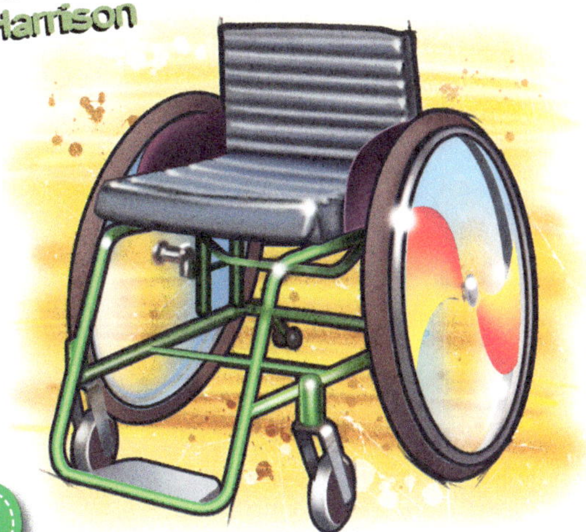

Contents

Chapter 1

A Big Game

On the morning of the big game, David showered quickly. He dressed quickly. He ate his breakfast quickly.

"Slow down!" laughed his mother. "You're buzzing about like a bumble bee in a bottle."

David laughed. "It's the best day of my life," he said. "It's my first ball game for the top team. I can't wait to get on the court."

The doorbell rang. It was David's friend Alex, who was in the team, too. David ate his last piece of toast and drank his juice.

"See you later, Mum," he called, as he ran out the door.

Chapter 2

The Accident

Seconds later, there was a loud screech of car brakes. Mrs Cooper didn't take any notice, as there were traffic lights outside their house. Cars often had to stop in a hurry. But, one minute later, her front door burst open.

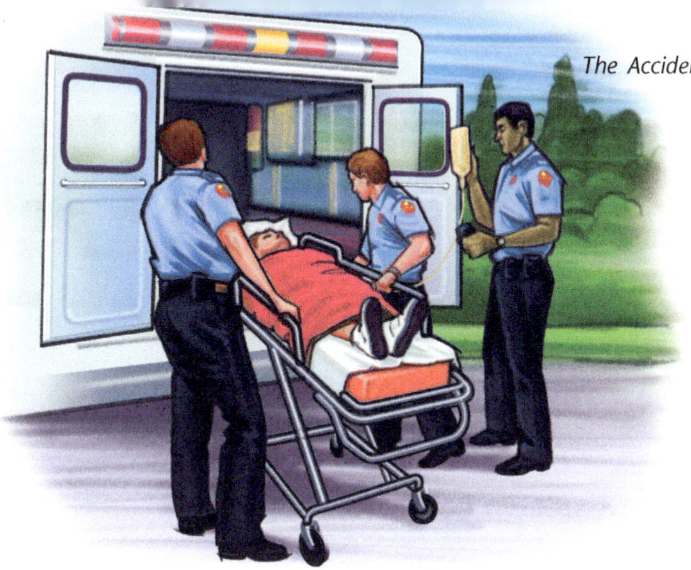

It was Alex. There were tears in his eyes. He could hardly speak. He pointed out the door.

"It's D-D-David," he stammered. "A car knocked him down."

Mrs Cooper reached David before the ambulance did. He was lying in a strange position. His legs were going the wrong way. He was unconscious. When the ambulance arrived, he was lifted onto a stretcher and taken to hospital.

Running Words 205

David was lucky to be alive. He was in a coma for six weeks. He stayed in hospital for nearly a year. When he came out, the top half of his body was as good as new. His brain was fine, and his arms were strong. But, his legs were too badly damaged to support him. He would be in a wheelchair for the rest of his life.

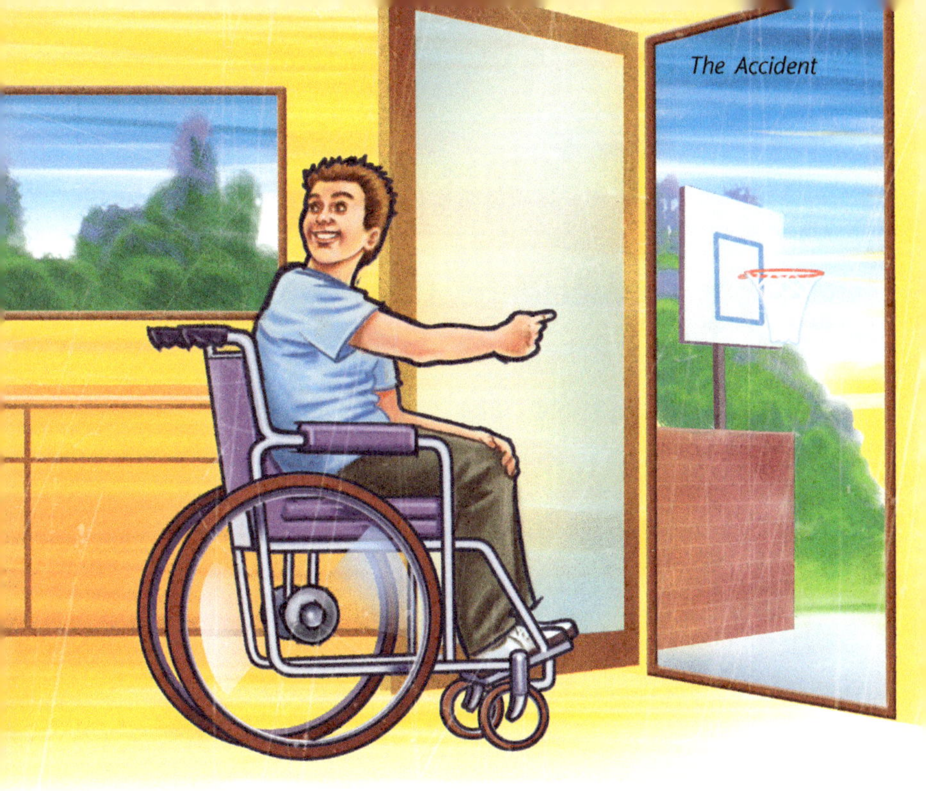

Alex visited David shortly after he came home.

"What shall we do?" Alex asked.

"Grab the ball," laughed David, wheeling his chair out the door. "Let's shoot some hoops."

Chapter 3

Changes

Before the accident, David was always in a hurry. After the accident, he was even worse. He raced around like a mad thing, in and out of the bathroom, up and down the passage, over to the fridge, up to the table, out the door. He was always at top speed.

"Slow down!" his mother laughed. "You're rushing around like a tornado. You're making me dizzy."

The accident changed David's life a lot, but there was a lot that didn't change. He couldn't run and jump and go rock-climbing any more. But, he could still shoot hoops, swim, wrestle with his friends and lift weights in the gym.

Most importantly, David could still play basketball. He joined the Wheelchair Cowboys and played goal attack for the C team.

"You're very good," the coach told him, "but you could be better. Practise your shooting. Strengthen your shoulders. Get really fit. You could be a champion if you try."

David practised shooting for hours. He pushed his wheelchair for miles, and lifted weights to build his arm muscles. He practised speed take-offs and fast turns. He was determined that one day he would play for the A team.

David got fitter, stronger, faster and more accurate with his shooting. He moved up to the B team.

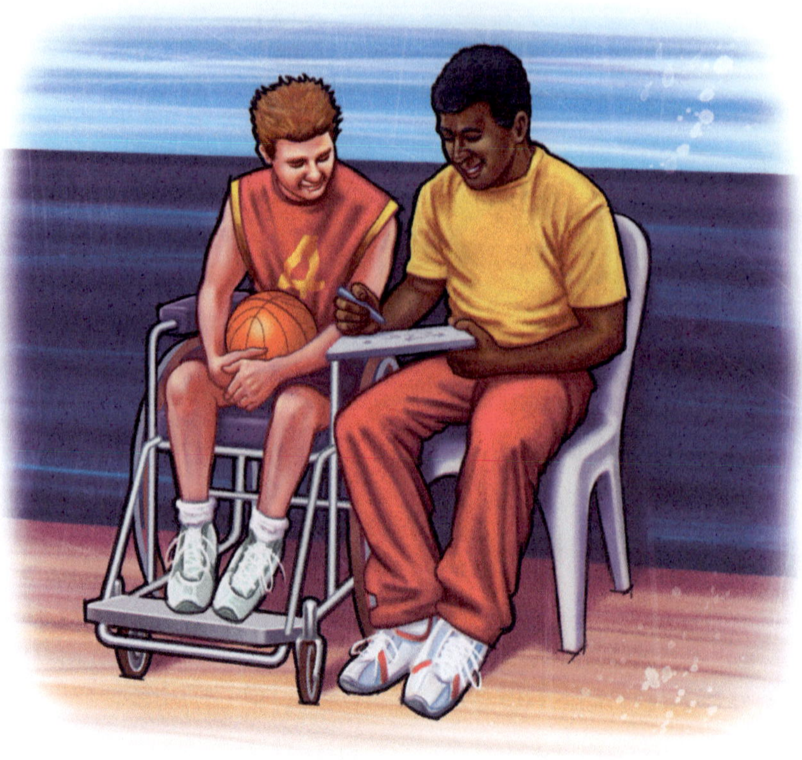

"Keep it up," said the coach. "You're big and strong. Your shooting is great, but you're slow around the court. It's your chair. It's not fast enough."

David wanted a new chair badly, but he didn't like to ask his parents for one. They had already spent a fortune on his hospital bills. They'd replaced the steps into their house with ramps. They'd changed his cupboards so he could reach his clothes. They'd even lowered the microwave so he could use it. He didn't like to ask for more.

One day, Mr and Mrs Cooper watched David and Alex racing home from school.

"That's not a wheelchair," laughed his dad. "It's more like a drag-racer. You go so fast I can smell the rubber tyres burning."

"Nah!" puffed David. "This wheelchair is as slow as a donkey with broken legs."

"It looks pretty quick to me," said his mum.

"I need a Zoomo really," said David. "Zoomos are sports chairs. They're designed for speed. They're light but strong. They're perfect for basketball, but they're expensive. This one's okay though."

Chapter 4

Surprise

"It's your turn to put the rubbish out," Dad said. "It's on the back ramp."

"Then come inside and do your homework," said Mum.

David and Alex went round the house to put out the rubbish. "Why didn't you say you need a new chair?" Alex asked David. "Don't you want to get into the A team?"

"It can wait," said David. Then he stopped. His mouth dropped open. His heart beat faster. He got tears in his eyes. There, in the middle of the path, was a brand new Zoomo Sports Chair.

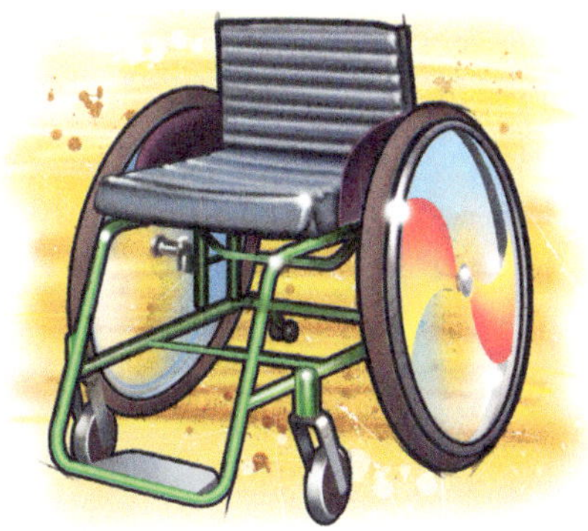

"Your parents are the greatest," said Alex.

"Yeah," agreed David. "The greatest!"

Chapter 5

Another Big Game

A month later, David woke up early on Saturday morning. He showered quickly. He dressed quickly. He gulped his breakfast down.

"This is the best day of my life," he told his mum. "My first game for the A Team."

"Slow down! Sit still!" laughed his mum. "You're jumping about like you've got ants in your pants."

But, she was too late. He was gone, out the door and away. Alex met him at the gate.

"Come on!" called David, racing down the footpath. "My game starts soon."

Alex ran to keep up. "It's still an hour away," he replied.

Chapter 6

Crash

When David and Alex reached the gym gate, David raced round the corner too quickly. His wheels went off the path.

Crash!

He fell down.

Thump!

He landed hard. He lay still. His eyes stayed closed.

"David!" yelled Alex. "Not again!" He grabbed his friend's arm. "Wake up! Can you hear me?"

There was no answer. "David! David! Wake up!" shouted Alex.

But David didn't wake up. He lay still.

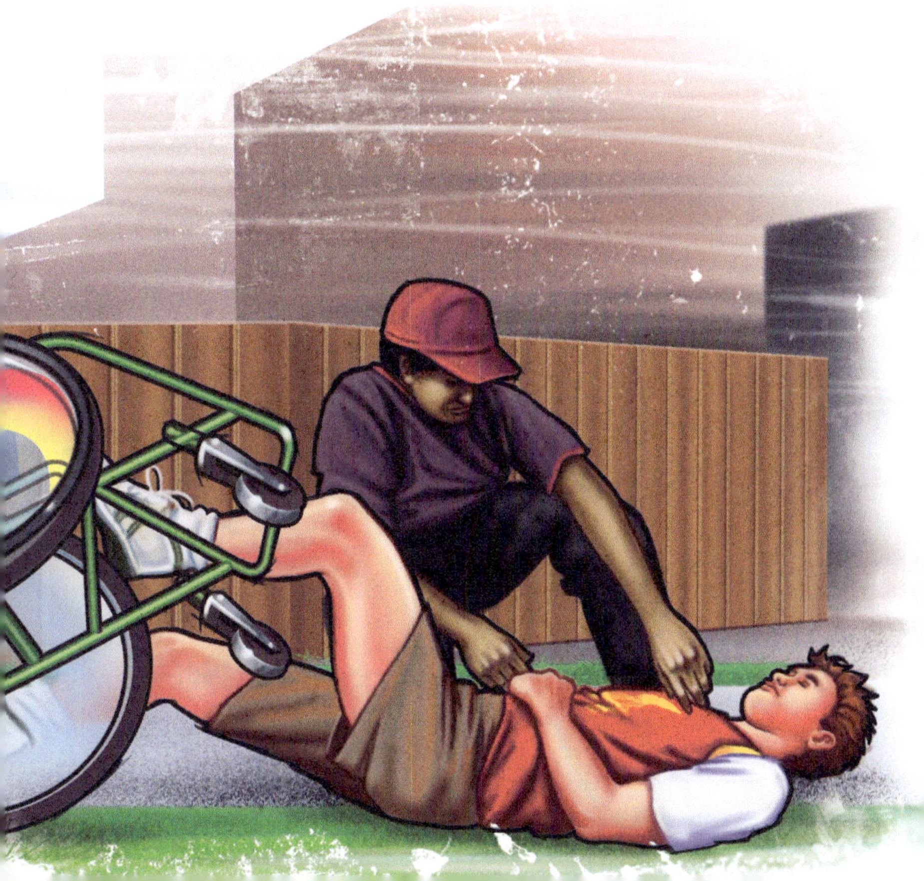

Then, David laughed. "I'm not hurt," he said. "I was just joking."

Alex laughed, too. "You gave me a fright," he said.

He stood the wheelchair up and David climbed back into it. He grinned at Alex.

"Thanks," he said. Then he sped off towards the gym. "Hurry up," he laughed back over his shoulder. "Do you always have to be so slow?"